S0-AIU-067

ALI
THE
GREAT

and the Eid Party Surprise

by SAADIA FARUQI   iLLustRated by DEBBY RAHMALIA

PICTURE WINDOW BOOKS
a capstone imprint

For Adam —SF
For Alesha —DR

Published by Picture Window Books, an imprint of Capstone
1710 Roe Crest Drive
North Mankato, Minnesota 56003
capstonepub.com

Text copyright © 2024 by Saadia Faruqi.
Illustrations copyright © 2024 by Capstone.

All rights reserved. No part of this publication may be reproduced in whole or in part, or stored in a retrieval system, or transmitted in any form or by any means, electronic, mechanical, photocopying, recording, or otherwise, without written permission of the publisher.

Library of Congress Cataloging-in-Publication Data
Names: Faruqi, Saadia, author. | Rahmalia, Debby, illustrator.
Title: Ali the Great and the Eid party surprise / written by Saadia Faruqi; illustrated by Debby Rahmalia.
Description: North Mankato, Minnesota : Picture Window Books, an imprint of Capstone, 2023. | Series: Ali the Great | Audience: Ages 5 to 8 | Audience: Grades K-1 | Summary: Second grader Ali Tahir is excited for the festival of Eid, and looking forward to the family party, but first he has to watch his little brother, Fateh, who is in a very cranky mood, and keeps throwing tantrums.
Identifiers: LCCN 2022048856 (print) | LCCN 2022048857 (ebook) | ISBN 9781666393897 (hardcover) | ISBN 9781484681251 (paperback) | ISBN 9781484681268 (pdf) | ISBN 9781484687543 (kindle edition) | ISBN 9781484681282 (epub)
Subjects: LCSH: Pakistani Americans—Juvenile fiction. | Id al-Fitr—Juvenile fiction. | Fasts and feasts—Islam—Juvenile fiction. | Brothers—Juvenile fiction. | Temper tantrums—Juvenile fiction. | CYAC: Pakistani Americans—Fiction. | Id al-Fitr—Fiction. | Brothers—Fiction. | Temper tantrums—Fiction.
Classification: LCC PZ7.1.F373 Al 2023 (print) | LCC PZ7.1.F373 (ebook) | DDC 813.6 [Fic]—dc23/eng/20221115
LC record available at https://lccn.loc.gov/2022048856
LC ebook record available at https://lccn.loc.gov/2022048857

Designers: Kay Fraser and Tracy Davies

Printed and bound in China. 5378

TABLE OF CONTENTS

I'M Ali Tahir, also KNOWN as

ALI
THE
GREAT!

And this is My family...

ABBA
doctor

AMMA
scientist

DADA
chief joke teller

DADI
best cook in
the world

FATEH
sneaky little brother

LET'S LEARN SOME URDU!

Ali and his family speak both English and Urdu, a language from Pakistan. Now you'll know some Urdu too!

ABBA (ah-BAH)—father (also baba)

AMMA (ah-MAH)—mother (also mama)

BHAI (BHA-ee)—brother

DADA (DAH-dah)—grandfather on father's side

DADI (DAH-dee)—grandmother on father's side

SALAAM (sah-LAHM)—hello

SHUKRIYA (shuh-KREE-yuh)—thank you

Chapter 1

EID DAY

Ali woke up bright and early.
"It's Eid day!" he shouted.

He got dressed and tidied his
room. Amma liked the whole
house to be clean for Eid. Ali
gathered up his juggling balls,
books, cars, and other toys and
shoved them under the bed.
Done!

Amma and Abba were

already in the kitchen. "Looks

like someone is excited," Amma

said, smiling.

Of course Ali was excited. Eid was the best day of the year! It came at the end of Ramadan. Eid meant visits with family and friends, and getting lots of presents.

Best of all, Ali's family always had an Eid party in the afternoon. It was going to be so much fun!

After breakfast, Ali raced back to his room to get dressed. He wore his new shalwar kameez and fancy shoes.

Dada met him downstairs.

"Looking spiffy," Dada said.

"We match!" Ali pointed out.

All the boys matched. Even

Fateh.

Amma showed Ali the henna

on her hands. It was beautiful.

"Wow!" Ali said.

"Me!" Fateh shouted. He

wanted henna on his hands too.

"Not for you," Ali told him.

"You're in charge of your little brother today," Amma reminded Ali.

"Yes, ma'am!" Ali replied.

Fateh pouted.

☆ Chapter 2 ☆

MISBEHAVING BROTHER

Fateh was in a cranky mood.

He cried as they drove to the

mosque to pray.

Ali's family prayed with their friends. Then they hugged each

other and said, "Eid Mubarak!"

Fateh ran around in the grass. He threw his goody bag on the ground and stomped on it. Then he cried because he'd broken his toys and candy.

"Behave, Fateh!" Ali whispered. "You're spoiling all the Eid fun."

"No!" Fateh shouted. Then he ran off with Ali's candy.

Ali sighed and went after his brother.

When they got home, it was
time to get ready for the Eid
party. Abba set up tables and
chairs in the backyard.

Ali helped.

Fateh didn't.

Amma brought out plates of food. "Our guests will be here soon," she said.

Fateh crawled under a chair and pretended to be a lion in a pen. "Roar!"

"Good kitty," Ali said.

Ali's friend Yasmin was the first to arrive. "Eid Mubarak!" she said. She handed Ali a giant box wrapped in colorful paper.

"Thanks!" Ali said and handed a present to Yasmin. "Amma says we can open gifts after dinner."

"Want to play tag?" Yasmin asked.

Just then, Fateh let out a cry as his chair tipped over.

Ali rolled his eyes. "Maybe later, Yasmin," he said.

☆ Chapter 3 ☆

JUGGLING FUN

Ali's parents were busy with the guests. Dada was on barbecue duty. Dadi was refilling water glasses. Ali was in charge of Fateh.

What would make his brother happy?

He thought of Fateh pretending to be a lion. That made him think of the circus. He snapped his fingers. "I'll be right back!"

He ran to his room and came back with a bag.

"Ladies and gentlemen!" Ali cried. "Welcome to Fateh's Eid Circus! It's time for Ali the juggler!"

All the kids sat and watched as Ali pulled three balls out of the bag. He tossed them high up in the air—one, two, three! Then he added one more.

The balls circled round and round as Ali juggled, higher and higher. He watched them carefully. Juggling was fun, but it took a lot of concentration.

"Ooh!" Fateh yelled. "Gimme!"

Ali tossed the balls high above his head one last time. Then, one by one, he caught them all and handed them to Fateh.

"You're so good at that!" Yasmin said.

Everyone clapped loudly. Ali grinned and bowed. "Thank you, thank you!" he said.

After dinner, Amma handed out a special Eid dessert called sawaiyan. It was Ali's favorite.

"Good job today," Amma whispered to him. Ali smiled.

Then it was time for the gift exchange. Ali got a magic show set, a jigsaw puzzle, and lots of books.

"Next Eid, you can add some magic tricks to your act," Dada said.

Ali looked at Fateh. "You can be my assistant," he said.

"Gimme!" Fateh said, and everyone laughed.

JUST JOKING AROUND

Why did the alien want to leave
the party?
The atmosphere wasn't right.

What do monsters serve at parties?
I-scream cake

Why did the elephant leave the circus?
He was tired of working for peanuts.

What sort of fish belongs in a circus?
A clown fish

EID MUBARAK!

Eid is an Arabic word meaning "festival" or "feast."

Muslims celebrate two Eids each year: Eid al-Fitr and Eid al-Adha.

Eid al-Fitr celebrates the end of Ramadan. Eid al-Adha marks the sacrifice of Abraham. Both are joyous occasions.

On Eid day, Muslims celebrate with prayer, food, family gatherings, and lots of fun!

During Eid, you can wish a Muslim "Happy Eid!" or "Eid Mubarak!"

THINK BIG WITH ALI THE GREAT!

☆ Ali's family celebrates Eid. Do you also celebrate Eid or have friends who do? What special days does your family celebrate?

☆ Ali's Eid celebration doesn't go exactly as he'd planned. Did you ever have someone spoil your fun? How did you handle it? Did you find a way to still enjoy the day?

☆ Have you ever been in charge of a younger sibling or relative? What advice would you give Ali to help with Fateh?

☆ About the Author ☆

Saadia Faruqi is a Pakistani American writer, interfaith activist, and cultural sensitivity trainer featured in *O, The Oprah Magazine*. Author of the Yasmin chapter book series, Saadia also writes middle grade novels, such as *Yusuf Azeem Is Not a Hero*, and other books for children. Saadia is editor-in-chief of *Blue Minaret*, an online magazine of poetry, short stories, and art. Besides writing, she also loves reading, binge-watching her favorite shows, and taking naps. She lives in Houston with her family.

☆ About the Illustrator ☆

Debby Rahmalia is an illustrator based in Indonesia with a passion for storytelling. She enjoys creating diverse works that showcase an array of cultures and people. Debby's long-term dream was to become an illustrator. She was encouraged to pursue her dream after she had her first baby and has been illustrating ever since. When she's not drawing, she spends her time reading the books she illustrated to her daughter or wandering around the neighborhood with her.

JOIN ALI THE GREAT
ON His Adventures!

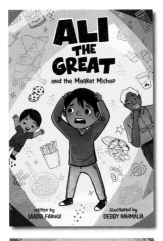

ALI THE GREAT and the Market Mishap

written by SAADIA FARUQI • illustrated by DEBBY RAHMALIA

ALI THE GREAT and the Dinosaur Mistake

written by SAADIA FARUQI • illustrated by DEBBY RAHMALIA

ALI THE GREAT and the Eid Party Surprise

written by SAADIA FARUQI • illustrated by DEBBY RAHMALIA

ALI THE GREAT and the Paper Airplane Flop

written by SAADIA FARUQI • illustrated by DEBBY RAHMALIA